Jess
Makes a
Promise

Collect all six Arctica Mermaid books

Also look out for the six original Mermaid SOS adventures in Coral Kingdom

Jess Makes a Promise

gillian shields

illustrated by helen Turner

BLOOMSBURY
CHILDREN'S
BOOKS

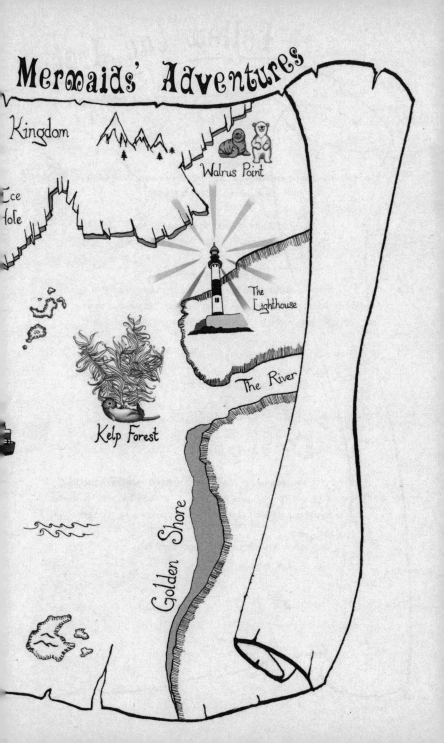

First published in Great Britain in 2007 by Bloomsbury Publishing Plc,
36 Soho Square, London, W1D 3QY

A CIP catalogue record of this book is available from the British Library

ISBN 978 07475 8971 6

Printed and bound in Great Britain by Clays Ltd, St Ives Plc

1 3 5 7 9 10 8 6 4 2

All papers used by Bloomsbury Publishing are natural, recyclable products
made from wood grown in well-managed forests. The manufacturing processes
conform to the environmental regulations of the country of origin.

www.bloomsbury.com/mermaidSOS

For Esme — *G.S.*

To my Uncle Jackie for his
love of art and encouragement
over the years

— *Love H.T.*

Prologue

When the evil mermaid, Mantora, tried
to destroy Coral Kingdom, she was
outwitted by Misty and her young
mermaid friends. Now she is hatching
another terrible plot! This time it is
against Ice Kingdom, the frozen realm
of Princess Arctica.

Mantora has stolen six precious Snow
Diamonds from the underwater Ice
Cavern. Not only that, she has trapped
Princess Arctica and her good Merfolk

in a huge cage of enchanted icicles, so they cannot follow her.

Unless the Snow Diamonds are quickly returned to the Ice Cavern, the whole of Ice Kingdom will be destroyed and the distant southern lands will be flooded with melted ice.

Only Princess Arctica's courageous young mermaids – Amber, Katie, Megan, Jess, Becky and Poppy – are small enough to slip through the jagged bars of Mantora's frosty cage. They are Sisters of the Sea, who are loyal to the Mermaid Pledge:

We promise that we'll take good care
Of all sea creatures everywhere.
We'll never hurt and never break,
We'll always give and never take.
And as we fight Mantora's threat,
This saying we must not forget:
'I'll help you and you'll help me,
For we are Sisters of the Sea!'

Amber and her friends vow to find the
Snow Diamonds, before their frosty home
melts for ever. They set off on their quest,
taking with them only Princess Arctica's
blessing and their Stardust Lockets.

Mantora has left behind a trail of
cryptic clues about where she has hidden
the Diamonds. Can Amber and her friends
solve Mantora's riddling rhymes and
rescue the Snow Diamonds in time to save
Ice Kingdom?

If you cannot find the Diamonds,
The ice will start to melt.
On all sides of the Ocean,
The danger will be felt.
No more will seals and polar bears
Enjoy their snowy home,
The seas will rise, the lands will flood –
Storm Kingdom will have come!
So try to solve the riddling clues
Of Mantora's cruel game,
But if you fail to work them out,
The world won't be the same ...

Jess

Chapter One

'Beachcomber, beachcomber,

Looking through the sand,

Find me a treasure

I can hold in my hand.

Beachcomber, beachcomber,

On your Island home,

Send me a message,

Through the waves and foam.

Beachcomber, beachcomber,

Hide the treasure deep below,
Where all the shrimps
And the angelfish go!'

Jess finished reading from the vivid orange scroll. She looked round at her mermaid friends – Amber, Katie, Megan, Becky and Poppy – who were gathered on the yellow sands of the Golden Shore.

'So what do you all think of the fourth clue?' Jess asked, sitting up on her sparkling turquoise tail. The young friends had to solve this rhyming riddle to find where Mantora had hidden the fourth Snow Diamond. Without the magical Diamonds, the mermaids' frosty home in Ice Kingdom would melt, and the world would be changed for ever.

'"*Beachcomber, beachcomber, looking through the sand...*"' repeated Becky dreamily, her silky black bun nodding in time to the words. 'It's not like the other clues, is it? It's really rather pretty.'

'Pretty!' exclaimed Poppy indignantly. 'How can anything to do with Mantora be pretty? Anyway, it doesn't matter whether the clue sounds nice – the important thing is what it means.'

The mermaids had already succeeded in finding three of the precious Snow Diamonds. They were now safely hidden in the Stardust Lockets hanging from the wrists of Amber, Katie and Megan. The Stardust Locket belonging to bold young Jess was in the shape of a lively dolphin. She was keen to find a Diamond to keep safe in her Locket as soon as possible.

'Poppy's right,' declared Jess. 'We must try to work out this clue straight away.' She looked at the orange scroll again, and studied the words carefully. 'Mantora has scribbled something at the bottom of the clue. Listen…

'You think you are so close to success, my meddling mermaids, don't you? But I promise that you are very far from the end of your quest. And I shall have a "whale" of a time watching your feeble struggles to solve this splendidly cunning clue...'

'What does she mean — a *"whale"* of a time?' puzzled Katie. 'Could that be something to do with Monty?'

The mermaids had been travelling by Whale Express, on the back of their friend Monty, a powerful humpback whale.

'No, it can't be,' replied Poppy. 'She's just laughing at us and being nasty as usual.'

'I'm not so sure, Poppy,' said Megan, with a thoughtful frown. 'I hope she isn't plotting something against poor Monty.'

Jess looked up boldly. 'If she tries to hurt Monty she'll have me to deal with, and that's a promise!' Jess had become firm friends with their faithful guide and companion. She loved to plunge through the waves, holding tightly to Monty's

broad back, as the wind ruffled her dark curls. 'But we should get away from this beach, before any Humans spot us. The morning sun is already high in the sky.'

'Good thinking,' said the others. 'Let's swim back to where Monty is waiting for us.'

With a powerful dive, Jess led the way through the clear waves. Soon, they found Monty, far out in the bay.

'So where are we off to next, Mermaids?' he asked good-humouredly.

'We're not sure yet,' said Jess. 'The clue is something to do with…wait…' She glanced at the scroll again, as she swished her tail in the water. 'We have to find a beachcomber!'

'That's someone who collects shells and pebbles from the shore,' said Amber. 'Maybe someone like that could pick up the missing Diamond?'

'That would fit in with the clue,' replied Katie.

The whale rolled over in the water, making a huge wave and a shimmering splash of spray. When he turned the right way again, he was grinning at his mermaid friends.

'I know something that would fit even better,' Monty said. 'The Beachcomber Islands! My folk swim there every year on their great travels.'

'That sounds perfect,' exclaimed Jess. '"*Beachcomber, beachcomber on your Island home*"…that must be the place!'

'And are there angelfish and shrimps there, like it says in the clue?' asked

Megan. Her pet Fairy Shrimp, Sammy, pricked up his feelers and listened eagerly.

'Hundreds,' replied Monty. 'Little Sammy will make lots of new friends. And there are so many other sea creatures too, living in the blue waters and coral reefs around the Beachcomber Islands. Not just angelfish, but butterfly fish, lizard fish, trumpet fish – and then there are the dolphins and seals and turtles…'

'Stop, stop! laughed Jess. 'You're making me feel dizzy.'

'It sounds marvellous,' breathed Becky, her eyes shining with delight. 'It sounds almost as good as the famous Coral Kingdom where Queen Neptuna lives. Oh, will you take us there, Monty?'

Soon, the young friends were holding tight to the whale's sleek back, ready and eager to set off.

'But remember that this isn't a holiday,' warned Amber. 'The Beachcomber Islands sound wonderful, but Mantora could be lurking anywhere, setting traps for us. And we still don't really know what the rest of the clue means. What about "*sending a message* and *hiding the treasure deep below*"?'

'We'll have to work that out later,' said Jess briskly. 'The first thing is to get there.

Come on, Monty – we're off to the Beachcomber Islands!'

The Whale Express was on its way again, taking the mermaids to exciting new places in the search for the fourth Snow Diamond. But what would the young friends find when they reached their destination?

Chapter Two

The mermaids were beginning to feel tired.
Their arms ached from clinging on to
Monty, as he sped towards the South. Even
Jess was starting to wonder if they would
ever get there. But suddenly Monty glided
to a stop in the deep blue sea. Brilliant
sunshine blazed in the bright sky.

'Here we are, Mermaids,' he announced.
'The Beachcomber Islands are ahead.'

One by one, the mermaids slid off his back into the waves, glad to be able to stretch their arms and ripple their tails freely once more. They looked up and shaded their eyes against the glare of the sun, curious to see the coral-ringed isles they had heard so much about.

'Wow!' said Jess. 'I can see them on the horizon. They look like green mountains

floating in the sea. There are two main Islands, a big one and a small one. Which one are we going to visit?'

'The Humans mostly live on the big Island,' replied Monty. 'So if the Beachcomber in your clue is a Human, perhaps you should start there.'

'But won't that be dangerous?' asked Becky cautiously. 'The Humans will have fishing boats going in and out of the harbour. We don't want them to catch us.'

'I'd like to see any fishing boat that could catch Monty,' laughed Jess, patting the whale's huge, sleek sides.

'Yes, just let them try!' grinned Monty. He raised his powerful tail, making sparkling spray fly all over the young friends.

'All the same we must be really careful,' said Amber sensibly. 'Now, which part of the Islands should we head for?'

But just then, the mermaids heard high, echoing voices floating on the breeze. They looked up and saw a pod of silvery dolphins leaping towards them. Each dolphin seemed to fly into the air, spinning round like a tornado before splashing back into the water.

'Spinner dolphins!' exclaimed Megan.

'Look, Sammy, they're so fast and elegant.'
Sammy the shrimp leapt from her hand
and tried to spin in the air, too.

'The dolphins are coming!' he squeaked.

Soon, Monty and the mermaids were
surrounded by a ring of friendly faces in
the warm blue waves.

'Greetings, Mermaids,' the dolphins

called. 'We
have been
looking for
you. You are
welcome to our
Island home.'

'Thank you,'
said Jess. 'But
why have you
been looking

for us? How did you know that we were here at the Islands? I thought our quest was a secret.'

'Not to Queen Neptuna,' the dolphins replied.

'Queen Neptuna!' cried Poppy.

'Yes, the great Queen herself is nearby,' said one of the dolphins, as she hovered in the water. 'My name is Soraya, and I have seen her with my own eyes. Queen Neptuna has travelled all the way from Coral Kingdom to give you something. She is waiting for you on the other side of the little Island.'

'Hooray!' shouted the mermaids. 'We're going to see Queen Neptuna!'

The friends hugged one another happily, cheering and laughing with excitement.

They could hardly believe this unexpected news.

'But don't you remember that Princess Arctica said she was going to get a message to the Queen?' Jess reminded them. 'Some swift birds must have flown to Coral Kingdom, telling Queen Neptuna of our quest.'

'And now she's here to help us,' said Katie and Megan, clasping their hands together in delight.

'Let's swim to the other side of the little Island straight away,' urged Amber.

'You too, Monty,' Jess added. 'Don't get left behind!'

The mermaids swirled their sparkling tails and got ready to dash away. But Becky hung back uncertainly. Her sensitive face looked troubled.

'Hurry up, Becky,' said Jess, noticing her friend. 'We mustn't be late for the Queen. Perhaps she already knows where the fourth Diamond is.'

But still Becky seemed reluctant to follow the others. She twisted her hands together nervously.

'What's the matter, Becky?' asked Jess curiously.

'I don't know,' Becky burst out in reply. 'The news that Queen Neptuna is here should fill me with joy. But my heart feels heavy, as though a dark cloud is passing over it. I don't think we should go to the other side of that Island.'

'Oh, poo!' said Poppy rudely. 'You're just being a silly scaredy-cat, Becky. We know you're frightened of being spotted by the Humans.' Poppy sometimes spoke before she thought, and her words tumbled out in an unkind rush. Becky blushed scarlet.

'I don't think I'm scared,' she protested, looking round at her friends with tears in her eyes. 'It just doesn't feel right, somehow.'

'Not right to do as your Queen commands?' questioned Soraya the dolphin. 'She told us with her own lips that she is waiting for you there. What can be the harm in that?'

Becky hung her head miserably, unable to put her feelings into words. Jess quickly put her arm round her friend to cheer her up.

'Don't worry,' she said kindly. 'You're probably just feeling nervous about meeting the Queen. Soraya's right – we must do as she says. You can hold my hand as we swim along, if that helps.'

40

Jess stuck her hand out with a smile. She never felt nervous about anything, but she was always ready to help anyone who did. Becky held Jess's hand gratefully and got ready to set off, still looking rather doubtful. Then the mermaids thanked the dolphins and dived into the turquoise

waves. Soon they were speeding away with
Monty to the far side of the smaller Island.

As they swam near, the young friends
could see that it was a lonely, wild place.
Its steep sides were covered in thick bushes
and palm trees and brilliant flowers. All
around the Island was a scattering of
rocks, their craggy heads poking up from

the deep blue sea. On the furthest of the rocks, the mermaids could see a mysterious figure, wrapped in a golden veil.

'That must be Queen Neptuna,' Jess called out in excitement. 'We're really going to meet her at last. This is going to be our lucky day!'

At least, that was what she thought…

Chapter Three

Jess and the mermaids swished their
glistening tails impatiently, and sped
towards the rock where the shrouded figure
sat. Monty glided behind them, smooth
and steady like a great ship. A sweet, rich
voice called out, 'Welcome, my dear Sisters
of the Sea. Come closer!'

In a few moments, the young friends
were looking up in wonder at the queenly

mermaid, who was perched on top of the rock. She seemed to be holding something behind her back. The mermaids could also see a sparkly crown twinkling beneath her long veil, but they could not see her face clearly.

'We have come as you asked…er…Your Majesty,' said Jess bravely. 'The dolphins said that you have something for us.'

'I have indeed,' said the mermaid, in a low voice. 'I have a wonderful… SURPRISE!'

With a sudden movement, she ripped off her veil, revealing not Queen Neptuna, but her fiendish sister, Mantora! Her dark hair blew around her deadly pale face, and her mouth was drawn back in a cruel smile. The little mermaids gasped in utter horror.

Mantora had tricked the dolphins with her cunning message, and now she had the Sisters of the Sea in her clutches.

'Ha, ha, ha!' shrieked Mantora, her voice no longer soft, but harsh and ugly. 'What a wonderful joke! Now you will give me those three Snow Diamonds back, and you will never find the others. How dare you try to defeat me, Mantora the Storm Queen?'

A crash of lightning tore through the sky, as the mermaids shivered in the shadow of the rock.

Mantora leaned over to snatch the
Stardust Locket from the mermaid nearest
to her. It was Becky, still clinging on to
Jess's comforting hand. But as Mantora's
bony fingers closed around the bracelet on
Becky's wrist, the look on the evil
mermaid's face changed from triumph to
pain.

'Eeeeooow!' she squealed, suddenly
letting go. The protective magic in Becky's
Stardust Locket had stung Mantora's
hand. As the mean-hearted mermaid
fussed over her sore fingers, Jess called out,
'Swim away, everyone! Swim back to
Monty!'

The mermaids desperately darted away
from the rock, but Mantora's cold voice
rang after them.

'There will be no escape for you on your precious Whale Express,' she hissed. 'Your foolish whale friend is about to be hunted down. I lured you all to this spot because I knew the whaling boat was about to pass by. And here it is!'

Jess whipped round in the water.

A heavy, hulking boat was coming into sight over the horizon. She could make out several tough-looking Humans on its decks, armed with guns and harpoons.

'It's a whaling boat,' she yelped in terror. 'They've spotted Monty. Dive, everyone! Monty! Get under the water quickly!'

Jess slithered below the waves. Her friends followed her, and they soon saw the dark outline of Monty ahead of them. He was gliding down to the bottom of the sea, just as Jess had urged him to do. The mermaids quickly rippled their tails and swam after him, until they all hovered together over the sea bed.

'Are you all right, Monty?' Jess asked.

'Yes I am,' said Monty, in a low rumble.

'But I won't be if that boat spots me on the surface.'

The mermaids looked up to the wide surface of the sea with anxious faces.

'Oh no,' whispered Megan. 'The boat is heading in our direction. We must stay here below the waves until it has gone.'

The friends clung together anxiously, waiting to see what would happen next.

'I wonder where Mantora is now?' shivered Becky.

'Let's hope she's not going to try any more of her wicked tricks,' Amber replied.

'She fooled all of us,' exclaimed Jess, 'pretending to be Queen Neptuna like that!'

'She didn't fool Becky,' said Poppy, in a small voice. 'Becky was the only one who saw through Mantora's plot.' The red-headed little mermaid blushed bright pink. 'I should think before I speak,' Poppy gulped. 'I'm sorry I was so mean to you earlier, Becky.'

'That doesn't matter,' said

Becky, squeezing Poppy's hand kindly. 'Just forget about it. The only thing that matters now is making sure that the whaling boat doesn't see Monty.'

The mermaids gathered round Monty, hoping that the boat would pass by. But it didn't. The dark shape of the whaler slowed down until it settled very near them. The Sisters of the Sea felt so worried. They knew that Monty would soon have to go up to the surface to breathe. But as soon as he did, the whalers would aim their deadly guns and harpoons at him, and there was nothing the mermaids could do to stop them.

'It makes me so cross that some Humans want to hunt the whales,' said Katie indignantly. 'Don't they know that the world needs Monty and his folk? When will they ever learn?'

'Oh, Monty,' sighed Jess, resting her curly head against her friend's smooth side. 'I wish Queen Neptuna really was here to help us. Whatever are we going to do?' But then she suddenly looked up, with a determined expression on her face. 'It's no good just sighing and wishing,' she declared. 'Queen Neptuna is far away, and Princess Arctica, too. They're relying on us

to sort out our own problems – and to solve the clues.'

'You're right, Jess,' said Amber. 'We have to come up with a plan ourselves.'

'I know,' replied Jess grimly. 'And I promise that I'm going to think of one!'

Chapter Four

Jess swam up and down, flicking her tail impatiently and muttering to herself. Monty began to look uncomfortable. He knew that he would have to go up to the surface to take a breath before long. As the minutes ticked by, Megan clasped her hands together nervously and murmured, 'This is just what Mantora wanted to happen when she tricked us into coming here.'

Jess snapped her fingers and cried, 'That's it, Megan! We need a trick, like Mantora used. The Humans are stronger than we are, and they have weapons to shoot and hurt Monty. We can't fight back with weapons, and we don't want to anyway. The Mermaid Pledge tells us that we should "never hurt". So we have to trick the boat into going away!'

'But how?' puzzled the mermaids.

'With the help of our friend Ana,' replied Jess. 'Amber, the last time you opened the

bag that she gave us, I noticed some
things in there that might be useful. Let's
have another look.'

Amber quickly passed the bag over to
Jess, who reached into the soft pouch and
lifted out six wonderful carvings. There
was a miniature Sea Lion, a Walrus, a
Beluga Whale, a Snowy Owl, a Golden
Fish and a noble Polar Bear – all creatures
from the mermaids' snowy home in Ice
Kingdom.

'Aren't they lovely?' said Becky
admiringly. 'Ana must have made them
herself.' The carvings were a bit like the
great statues back home in the Ice Cavern,
but they were made from polished
driftwood instead of ice. The Inuit folk
were skilled in this craft, and Ana had

captured the creatures' spirits perfectly.

'But how can these tiny things help me?' asked Monty doubtfully. 'It's not as though we have an army of the creatures.'

'No, we don't,' replied Jess, with a grin. 'Not yet, at least. You stay down here, Monty. But I'm going up to the surface with Ana's carvings. *Mermaid SOS!*' She clutched the little statues and raced away in a trail of silver bubbles, before the

others could say anything.

'Wait, Jess,' they cried. 'It's too much of a risk, going up there!'

The daring young mermaid looked back over her shoulder at her friends and called out, 'I don't care! I'd do anything to try to save Monty, even if it is dangerous.'

Amber and the others looked at one another helplessly.

'We can't let her do this on her own,' said Amber, with a swish of her lilac tail. 'We're a team, and Monty is our friend, too. Come on, everyone — *Mermaid SOS!*'

The brave young friends dashed after Jess, shooting through the water like a rainbow. 'But don't show yourself to the whalers, anyone,' called Katie. 'Be careful!'

Very soon, the mermaids were peeping

above the blue waves. On one side of them, the Islands rose up like green mounds. On the other, the boat loomed ahead. They could see two men handling a deadly harpoon and scanning the sea for any sign of Monty.

'So what's the plan, Jess?' asked Poppy, as they tried to keep out of sight of the hunters.

'Here, take one of the carvings each,' whispered Jess, handing them out to her

friends. 'Now hold them up. We're going
to give these whalers the fright of their
lives.'

The mermaids held up the Inuit statues,
as Jess began to sing:

> *'Creatures of our snowy home,*
> *We need your spirits now to roam*
> *Far across the warm blue sea,*
> *To help dear Monty to be free.*
> *Stardust Lockets, we need your power*
> *In this dark and dangerous hour.*
> *So conjure up an army here,*
> *To fill the whalers' hearts with fear!'*

Softly, the mermaids began to chant over
and over again, '"*Conjure up an army
here…fill the whalers' heart with fear…*"'

As they did so, a stream of silver sprinkles fell from their Stardust Lockets on to the carvings.

The little statues began to glow, then shine, then sparkle, and suddenly from each one a huge shape sprang up. From Jess's carving the shimmering mirage of an enormous Polar Bear rose and settled on the waves like a ghost. Then all the carvings produced their own eerie spirit creatures, until the sea surged with the enchanted shapes of a massive Sea Lion, a Walrus, a Beluga Whale and a Golden Fish. A giant Snowy Owl swooped through the air above them.

'CHARGE!' shouted Jess, at the top of her voice.

At that instant, the ghostly Polar Bear

began to gallop across the waves towards the black sides of the boat, followed by the rest of the mysterious horde. The men on deck looked up when they heard the noise, thinking that they would soon be catching a fine whale. But when they saw the army of enormous spirit creatures hurtling towards them, the expressions on their faces changed to total terror. They couldn't believe their eyes.

'C-can you see what I see?' one of them moaned.

'I see g-g-*ghosts!*' the other man stuttered. 'And they're huge! That's the end of hunting for me today!'

The terrified whalers threw down their weapons, and then the whole crew began to panic. They rushed to turn the vessel around and get away as quickly as possible. Soon, the whaling boat was nearly out of sight.

'Hooray!' cried the mermaids. 'Thank you, Stardust Lockets! Thank you, spirits of the sea! And three cheers for Jess!'

Chapter Five

The glowing shapes of the enchanted sea creatures rapidly began to shrink and fade. Soon, they returned into the little carvings, leaving nothing behind but a few silver sprinkles of Stardust…

'Let's go and tell Monty it's safe for him to come up now,' said Jess, with a relieved smile. But just then, the whale's huge head appeared above the waves. Monty blew out a tall tower of spray, and then took a huge breath.

'Sorry!' he panted. 'But I couldn't stay underwater any longer. I did need that gulp of air. Jess, you put yourself in danger to keep your promise to save me. You're a true friend.'

'Thank you, Monty,' beamed Jess,

cuddling her cheek against Monty's sleek face. 'I'm so glad those greedy hunters have gone.'

'But other boats might be on their way,' warned Katie. 'Let's sink down out of sight again, just in case.'

'And we *must* start thinking about the fourth clue,' said Amber. 'Don't forget we made a promise to Princess Arctica, too.'

The mermaids looked serious again. Mantora hadn't succeeded in harming Monty, but she had certainly delayed their quest.

'Put your thinking caps on, everyone,' cried Jess, as the friends plunged down towards the sea bed. 'How are we going to find the fourth Diamond – and in double quick time?'

The mermaids quickly settled on the rocky sea bed, curling their glistening tails under them, while Monty rested nearby.

'Didn't the clue say something about treasure?' asked Katie. 'That must be the Diamond.'

'And there was something about a message,' added Becky.

'Don't forget the bit about the angelfish,' said Megan.

'And the shrimps!' squeaked Sammy.

'Did I hear someone looking for shrimps and angelfish?' called out a voice behind them. 'Then you've come to the right place.'

A colourful angelfish glided into view. His slim, flat body was a brilliant orange, with pearly blue markings. Jess and the others turned to greet him with friendly smiles. But when the angelfish saw them, his mouth dropped open in dismay. He waggled his whole body fiercely at them.

'So you're mermaids, are you?' he growled. 'I'm Archie, and I warn you that I've had enough of your kind. Be off with you, we don't want you here!'

'But whatever's wrong?' asked Jess, her brown eyes growing wide in astonishment.

The mermaids had never met anyone so cross before! It was very strange, and they felt very puzzled.

'We haven't done anything to hurt you,' said Poppy cheekily.

69

'Why are you being so unfriendly?'

'Because of that nasty mermaid who was lurking here last night,' scowled Archie.

'Mantora!' chorused the mermaids, glancing quickly at one another.

'Aha, so you do know her,' Archie shouted. He darted about angrily, his orange body flashing through the water like a bright flag. 'I suppose she's a friend of yours?'

'No, she isn't,' shuddered Jess. 'In fact, she's our greatest enemy.'

As Jess explained how Mantora had tried to lure Monty into the path of the whaling boat, Archie began to calm down.

'Really?' he said. 'Then you know how terrible she is. Why, she even laughed when she saw what had happened to our poor coral – and just look at it!'

Jess and her friends glanced around the sea bed. They soon noticed that the coral, which should have been beautiful shades of red and green and orange, was white. It stuck up from the sea bed like a ghostly skeleton.

'But why is the coral like that?' gasped the mermaids. 'What happened to it?'

'It's because the waters round here are

getting too warm for our delicate coral,'
sighed Archie. 'Its wonderful colours have
been bleached away by the warm water.
And if the water gets even warmer, this
coral will die completely. Where will
we angelfish live then? And what will
happen to the sea stars, and the anemones,
and all the other creatures of the coral?'

'Oh, we *must* get the Snow Diamonds
home to Ice Kingdom,' said Jess urgently.
'If Ice Kingdom melts there will soon be no
coral left at all. But if we can keep Ice
Kingdom cool and frosty, perhaps this
coral will get better.'

Then Jess quickly told Archie all
about the Snow Diamonds and their
quest to find them. 'But Mantora is
doing her best to stop us getting them

72

back,' she added, with a sigh.

'Mantora again!' spluttered the indignant little fish. 'Wasn't I telling you that she was here only last night? She was riding on the back of a monstrous green sea serpent, poking around down here, getting up to no good. And she nearly terrified poor Sonny to death.'

'Who is Sonny?' asked Becky with a shiver, not liking the sound of Mantora's sea serpent. She and Megan held hands rather nervously, as they listened to the angry angelfish.

'He's my best friend,' explained Archie. 'Sonny's a little shrimp, and when he saw Mantora's sea serpent, he darted behind those rocks over there. He hasn't dared to come out since.'

'Have you really got a friend who's a shrimp?' said Megan, with pink cheeks and sparkling eyes. 'So have I – this is Sammy!'

Sammy waved his feelers to say 'hello', as he sat on Megan's shoulder.

'Sonny will want to meet you, Sammy,' said Archie, cheering up a bit. 'I'll go and see if I can persuade him to come out now.'

He instantly zigzagged through the clear water, over to the rocks.

'I wonder what Mantora was looking for,' said Becky thoughtfully, as the mermaids waited for Archie to come back.

'It must have been something to do with the Diamonds,' said Katie. 'Jess, let's see that clue again.'

Jess quickly found the roll of orange parchment and smoothed it out. The mermaids gathered round to study the riddle, and Amber murmured, '"*Hide the treasure deep below, Where all the shrimps And the angelfish go!*"'

'Well, that's here by the coral, isn't it?' Jess exclaimed. 'This is where the shrimps and the angelfish live.'

'And if the treasure is the Diamond...' said Megan.

'...then Mantora must have buried it down here last night,' finished Poppy. 'She wasn't looking for something, she was *hiding* something.'

The little mermaids felt thrilled to be on the trail of the Diamond at last.

'So what are we waiting for?' asked Jess.

'Let's start digging!'

Jess and her friends
started to scrape
away at the sea bed
with their bare
hands. Even Monty
joined in, scooping
up sand with his

strong tail. When Archie returned a few
minutes later, he stared at them in
astonishment.

'What are you doing, Sisters of the Sea?'
he asked. A timid red shrimp swam closely
behind him, peering round nervously for
any sign of Mantora and her sea serpent.

'We're digging for treasure,' panted Jess.

'But that's not where the treasure is,'
piped Sonny, the tiny shrimp. Then he

blushed at his own boldness and muttered, 'Everyone round here knows that.'

Now it was the mermaids' turn to be surprised.

'What do you mean, Sonny?' asked Megan gently.

'Tell them about the treasure chest, Archie,' Sonny replied, hiding behind his friend, and glancing shyly at Monty and the mermaids.

'Yes, do tell us,' pleaded Jess. The mermaids listened expectantly, as the angelfish began his tale...

Chapter Six

'Long, long ago, there was a shipwreck near this reef,' Archie explained. 'Over the years, the Humans from the Islands dived down many times to take away the valuable cargo. But there was one old chest that they never found. It's half buried by the rocks over there. I've never seen inside it, as the lid is too heavy for me to lift. But that's surely the spot to look for this treasure of yours.'

'Can you show it to us?' cried the mermaids.

'Sonny will lead the way,' said Archie. 'You don't have to be shy, Sonny. These young Sisters of the Sea are nothing like that dreadful Mantora!'

The little shrimp puffed out his chest bravely and sped away, his dainty legs pedalling swiftly through the water. Sammy followed him closely, as Monty, Archie and the mermaids glided along behind. Jess felt her heart beating with excitement. At last, the friends reached a big black rock on the sea bed.

At the foot of the rock, half hidden by the sand, was a rusty iron chest. It was covered in limpets and seaweed. A shaft of light from the Overwater world struck its old metal hinges and made them gleam. The chest looked the perfect hiding place for a stolen Diamond. Jess and her friends pulled eagerly at the heavy lid. It groaned and creaked spookily. Slowly, slowly, the chest began to open, and the mermaids saw...

'Nothing!' yelped Poppy. 'It's empty!'

'Wait,' said Jess. 'There's something tucked in the corner.'

She lifted out a bundle of rags. Wrapped inside the tattered material was a tarnished silver penny and a smoky glass bottle.

'Just some rubbish, left from the old days,' said Poppy in disgust. 'Everything else that was in the chest has rotted away in the water.'

'I like this bottle though,' said Sammy brightly. 'It would make a good hiding place for a shrimp.' He and Sonny swam down the bottle's long green neck, then wriggled out again. 'That was fun,' Sammy said. 'Do you think we could keep this? I could ride in it like a little boat, floating over the waves.'

'Sammy, you're a genius,' exclaimed Jess. 'You've just given me an idea!'

'Have I?' replied Sammy, looking confused. Jess turned to the others with a flushed, eager face.

'I've heard stories about bottles travelling over the waves, just like Sammy said,' Jess explained excitedly. 'But they had something special in them — messages!'

'Of course!' gasped Becky. 'A message in a bottle would be sent *"through the waves and foam"*, just like the clue said. That must be what we have to find, not buried treasure in a chest.'

'And the message in the bottle will be the fourth Diamond and the next clue,' said Katie, with shining eyes. 'Mantora must have hidden it near here, when she was hanging about last night. Oh, well done Jess, you've solved the clue at last!'

She caught hold of Jess's hands and did a wild Mermaid Dance in the water. Everyone joined in, laughing and smiling. Even Sammy and Sonny waved their feelers joyfully.

'But we still don't know where that bottle is,' added Amber breathlessly, when they all tumbled back down to the sea bed. 'Wherever could it be?'

'I've got an idea about that,' grinned Jess. 'Follow me!'

With a flurry of sparkling tails and silver bubbles, the friends followed Jess up to the surface once more. They looked around with relief. The sun was shining and there was no sign of the whaling boat – or of Mantora.

'Where are you taking us, Jess?' asked Katie, shaking her long plait over her shoulder.

'Back to that rock where we saw Mantora,' replied Jess,

as they all plunged through the waves.
'I've remembered something important.
I'm sure she was hiding something behind
her back, before she attacked us. We must
look by that rock very carefully. I've got a
feeling Mantora might have left something
there…'

Soon, the mermaids were swimming
near the sunny rock where Mantora had
tried to trick them, searching intently for
any sign of the precious Diamond. The
seawater swirled in little currents and
eddies. Scraps of driftwood churned up and
down on the waves, getting caught by the
rock before they floated away again.

Sammy and Sonny suddenly darted
forwards. Knocking gently against the
rock, held in place by a craggy spur, was a

shiny object that glinted in the sun. With a great heave, the shrimps lifted an ancient-looking bottle over their heads. Then they skimmed back through the water, coming to a halt in front of Jess.

'Is this the treasure that you're looking for, Sisters of the Sea?' they chirped.

Jess was dazzled by a thousand sparks of light shining through the bottle's glassy sides.

'I can see it!' she exclaimed. 'The fourth Diamond is hidden in the bottle, just like we thought. Mantora must have dropped it into the sea when she was talking to us. It was there all the time, waiting for someone to find it. Thank goodness we got there before anyone else did.'

'Good old Jess,' cried the mermaids. 'You worked it out so cleverly.'

The friends sank safely under the waves once more, very glad to have found the 'treasure' at last.

'But I couldn't have found the Diamond without Archie and Sonny,' Jess smiled. 'And now we're one step nearer to helping your bleached coral to get better again, Archie.'

'I'm happy we could help,' Archie replied. 'I'm just sorry I wasn't very friendly when we first met.'

The angelfish looked rather ashamed, and he wriggled uncomfortably from side to side in the clear water.

'That's all right, Archie,' said Jess. 'Mantora stirs up distrust wherever she goes.'

'Will you promise me one thing, now

that we are friends?' Archie asked, looking up eagerly.

'Of course,' chorused the mermaids.

'Promise that you will find the other Snow Diamonds as quickly as you can,' he begged. 'That way Ice Kingdom will be safe and our seas will not get any warmer. Do what you can to save our coral!'

'We promise,' replied Jess solemnly. 'And now it's time for us to carry on with our quest.'

The Sisters of the Sea said farewell to their new friends, and Sammy waved all his feelers and legs at once as he said goodbye to Sonny.

'Goodbye, Archie!' they cried. Hope filled the mermaids' hearts once more, as they watched the angelfish and the tiny shrimp swim happily down to the sea bed. It felt good to know that another Snow Diamond was safe.

Then the brave young mermaids clustered round Monty, ready to speed away to the next part of their adventure. But first, Jess carefully broke the seal on the bottle, and let the Diamond slide out on to her hand. It glittered and glimmered like a magical splinter of ice, twinkling purple and silver and white. Jess hid the marvellous jewel safely in her Stardust Locket.

'There!' she said, with a satisfied air. 'Mantora's horrible plot to hurt Monty has failed, we made some new friends and we have four Snow Diamonds! I think we're doing rather well, don't you?'

'That depends on what the next clue says,' said Becky.

'This yellow parchment tucked inside the bottle must be clue number five,' said Jess. 'Why don't you read it to us, Becky, so that we can find out?' Then she handed the bottle over, feeling confident that the end of their quest was in sight at last.

But as Jess and her friends waited hopefully to hear the fifth clue, they didn't know that Mantora was planning something totally unexpected for the Sisters of the Sea. It was something that might ruin their mission for ever...

Amber has golden curls and a gleaming lilac tail. She looks after her friends, and is a good leader.

Katie enjoys playing her Mermaid Harp. She has a long plait over her shoulder and a sparkly lemon-coloured tail.

Megan has sweet wavy hair and a spangled pink and white tail. She is never far from her pet Fairy Shrimp, Sammy.

Jess is bold and brave, with dark curls and a dazzling turquoise tail. She is friends with Monty, the humpback whale.

Becky loves the beauty of the sea. Her hair is decorated with flowers, and her tail is a pretty peach colour.

Poppy has coppery curls, a bright blue tail, and bags of confidence, but her impatience can land her in trouble.